P9-DGP-845

the Lost-and-Found tooth

ALSO BY LOUISE BORDEN AND ADAM GUSTAVSON

The John Hancock Club
The Last Day of School
The A+ Custodian
The Day Eddie Met the Author
Good Luck, Mrs. K.!

Margaret K. McElderry Books
An imprint of Simon & Schuster Children's Publishing Division
1230 Avenue of the Americas, New York, New York 10020

Book design by Sonia Chaghatzbanian
The text for this book is set in Carre Noir.
The illustrations for this book are rendered in watercolor.
Manufactured in China
2 4 6 8 10 9 7 5 3 1
Library of Congress Cataloging-in-Publication Data
Borden, Louise.
The lost-and-found tooth / Louise Borden.—1st ed.
p. cm.
Summary: A special calendar hangs in Mr. Reilly's second-grade classroom, and Lucy Webb impatiently awaits the day when she can add her name for losing a tooth, but when her time arrives, something unexpected happens.
ISBN-13: 978-1-4169-1814-1
ISBN-10: 1-4169-1814-0
[1. Teeth—Fiction. 2. Schools—Fiction. 3. Lost-and-found possessions—Fiction.] I. Title.
PZ7.B64827Lo 2008
[Fic]—dc22
2006028761

For Emma Dryden
—L. B.

For Steph
—A. G.

the Lost-and-Found tooth

written by
Louise Borden

illustrated by
Adam Gustavson

MARGARET K. MCELDERRY BOOKS
New York London Toronto Sydney

Mr. Reilly's Tooth Calendar

When West Street Elementary began in August,
every second grader in Room 19
had already lost some baby teeth.

Everyone but me.
I hadn't lost *one*.

My friend Tuck
had lost three.
Claire had lost five.
And Eduardo,
who sat next to me,
had lost *seven*.

I could ice skate without falling,
I could name the fifty states,
and I could spell *Tyrannosaurus Rex*.
But I couldn't lose a tooth.

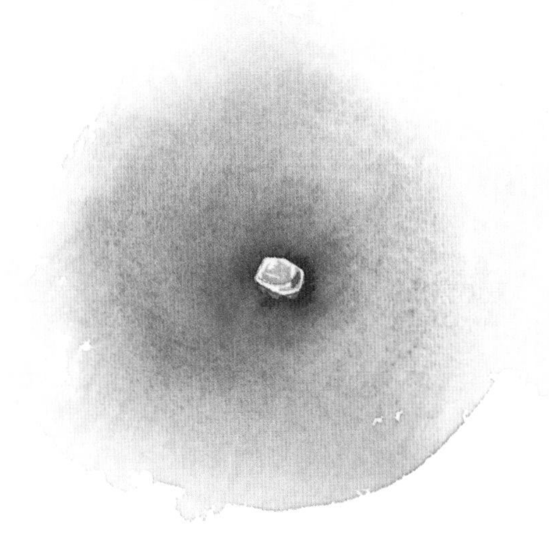

During the first week of second grade,
our teacher, Mr. Reilly,
kept us so busy reading good books
that I didn't have time
to think about losing teeth.

Chapter books were our favorites.
And mysteries.
And stories about animals
and friends.

Then Charlie Emerson lost a tooth.

He was the first person in our class
who got to write on Mr. Reilly's
WHO'S LOST A TOOTH? calendar.

Charlie had been wiggling his tooth
with his tongue
back and forth, back and forth,
all morning during Language Arts.
Finally he clicked it loose
when our class was hurrying
in our quiet-as-Reilly-mice line
down the hallway to Gym.
That afternoon
we crowded around Charlie
and watched as he wrote

Charlie – August 30th, 10:50 a.m. going to gym

on the calendar
using Mr. Reilly's special green marker
that had a plastic tooth on the end.

Mr. Reilly's rule
was that we had to record
the date, time, and place
where the wiggly tooth had been lost.

"Knowing the date
and telling time
and sharing stories
are second-grade skills
that are *quite* important,"
our teacher said
as he loosened his tie.

Mr. Reilly always loosened his tie
when he told us things
he wanted us to remember.

Then in September,
Vijay jiggled his tooth out
during soccer practice.
"It didn't even bleed,"
he told us the next day.
Again, the class crowded around
and watched as he wrote
on the tooth calendar:

Vijay, September 16, 4:20 p.m. Soccer Field,
playing goalie

Everyone in the class had at least one loose tooth
and knew their turn would come.
Everyone but me.

Tooth Math

At the beginning of November,
Mr. Reilly pointed to each month
on the tooth calendar.

"We set a losing record last month!
More students lost a tooth in October
than in September or August.

Let's count up the names. . . .
How many students lost a tooth in the A.M.?

In the P.M.?

How many girls lost a tooth in October?

And how many boys?

How many more students lost teeth in October
than in September?

Than in August?"

CALENDA

Name	Date	Time	Where?
Patty	October 3	2:06 p.m.	Fishing with my dad
Claire	October 8	11:20 AM.	In the school library
HENRY	OCTOBER 9	8:10 a.m.	ON THE SCHOOL BUS
Juan	October 15	11:38 a.m.	In the lunch line
Tuck	October 20	7:30 a.m.	Brushing my teeth
LOUISE	OCTOBER 26	1:19 P.m.	IN SOCIAL STUDIES
SAM	OCTOBER 31	5:20 P.M.	IN MY COUNT DRACULA COSTUME

Mr. Reilly always made math problems
seem as easy as pie.
But I wanted my name to be counted too.

I wore a red wristwatch
every day now,
just to be ready
for my turn at the calendar.

Tooth Stories

In Mr. Reilly's classroom
everyone's lost tooth told a story.

"Around the world at this very moment
there are second graders
whose baby teeth are being wiggled and lost,"
said Mr. Reilly.
"*Thousands* of second-grade tooth stories—
every day!"

He loosened his tie and said:
"Even astronauts headed to the moon,
and movie stars on the big screen,
and the writers of those books we love
lost their baby teeth when they were your age.
Think about that."

Patty raised her hand and said:
"I think there must be a *bazillion* tooth stories
in the world!"

We all knew she was right.

Every few weeks
there was a new lost-tooth story
that someone shared in Room 19.

In November
three more kids signed their names
on the WHO'S LOST A TOOTH? calendar.

PETER NOVEMBER 6 8 AM. ZIPPING MY COAT
Shelley November 23 5:05 pm Eating popcorn/reading a book
Cate November 27 4:41pm Biking to Ian's House

Was I *ever* going to lose a tooth
and have a story to tell?

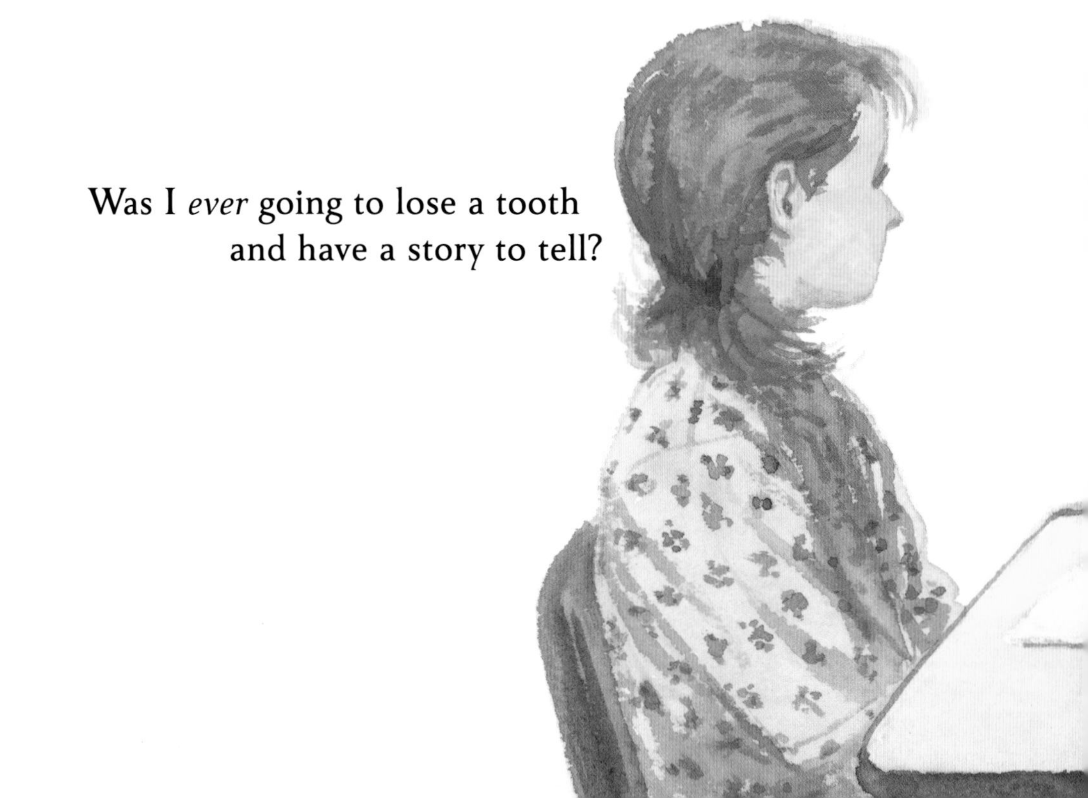

WHO'S LOST
A TOOTH?
CALENDAR
September

Second-Grade Stuff

Mr. Reilly was always reminding our class
that second grade was more
than just having smiles
with missing teeth.

"In second grade
we're thinkers and explorers and builders.
We have big ideas in Room 19."

We learned about plains and rivers
and mountains and oceans.
We painted our own landform maps,
which we made with dough.

Mr. Reilly read us one hundred good poems . . .
and then we wrote our own.
We taped them all over West Street Elementary
to share the ones we loved best.

One week in February,
we learned what the word *biography* meant,
and we dressed up as past presidents.
I was William Howard Taft.
He was our largest president.
I wore my dad's bow tie, his vest,
and his business suit jacket,
and I carried my grandpa's fancy pocket watch.

Tuck was Andrew Jackson.
He put down his sign that said OLD HICKORY
and helped me stuff a pillow
under my costume
just before our Parade of the Presidents began.

That was when I finally
felt one of my bottom teeth wiggle . . .
just a teeny, tiny bit.
First I felt it with my tongue,
and then I pushed it with my finger.

"Look, Tuck!
My tooth is loose!"
I opened my mouth
and let Tuck peek inside.
He pushed my tooth with his finger.

Then he nodded and said,
"*That* is a loose tooth, Lucy."

During our parade
I had the biggest smile
of all the presidents
in Mr. Reilly's class.

When we got back to Room 19,
I showed my loose tooth to Harry S. Truman,
who was really Claire.

I asked her how soon
my tooth would fall out,
and she said,
"Not today. It'll take a while."

I didn't care.
I'd been a president in a parade
and my first tooth was loose,
all in the same day.

Mr. Reilly's Surprise

The next Monday,
after the principal, Ms. Ireland,
made her morning announcements,
Mr. Reilly gathered our class together on the rug.

"My wife and I were cleaning out our attic,
and I found a box of things
from when I was in elementary school.
I've got *positive proof*
that I was once a second grader."

We all knew what the word *proof* meant
because we'd learned how to look for clues
in the mystery books we read.

Mr. Reilly held up a faded yellow report card:

JAMES REILLY—GRADE 2—GREENFIELD ELEMENTARY SCHOOL

Our class scooted closer
to see the old report card.

"Cool!"
"Look at that!"

Maddie asked, "What was your teacher's name?"
Juan asked, "What was your favorite subject?"
And I asked, "Did you ride a bus to school?"

"Miss Winslow . . .
Art and Recess . . .
walked seven blocks, rain or shine . . . ,"
answered Mr. Reilly.

Then he reached into his pocket,
pulled out a little box,
and said,
"*This* is what I really want to show you."

He opened the lid
and inside the box was . . .
a *tooth*!

Mr. Reilly's tooth!
It was a tiny tooth.
A baby tooth!
It was much too small
to fit inside Mr. Reilly's wide smile.

"Look at that tooth!" said Eduardo.
"Is that *really* your tooth?" asked Patty.
"I bet it *smells* now . . . ," said Sam.
Everybody laughed.

Mr. Reilly put the tooth on his desk
and then unfolded a scrap of paper
from the box.

"Lucy Webb,
why don't you come up and read this aloud for us,"
he said.

I squinted at the words.
The printing was messy—
not like Mr. Reilly's neat teacher handwriting.

First tooth. Second grade.
Lost on April 20, 4:12 p.m.
Playing baseball with Tony.

"Who's Tony?" asked Vijay.
"Tony's my big brother," said Mr. Reilly.
"He's two years older."

"Do you *remember* losing that tooth,
Mr. Reilly?" I asked.
"You bet, Lucy," he said.
"I was catching a pop fly.
I was so happy to *finally* lose a tooth!"
Mr. Reilly gave a wink
that I knew was just for me.

"I hope mine will come out soon," I said.
"When your tooth *does* come out,"
said Mr. Reilly, loosening his tie,
"you'll have a good story."

A Recess Story

My bottom tooth got looser
and looser
and looser.

Then on a cold sunshiny day,
in the middle of recess,
I was playing tag with Claire and Tuck.
I was the chaser,
and we were running around
clumps of melting snow
on the wet blacktop.

My shoelace came undone,
and when I stopped to tie my shoe,
I put my hand in my mouth to wiggle my tooth
and suddenly
there it was
stuck on my blue mitten!

I'd lost a tooth!
I'd lost my *first* tooth!

Right away
I looked at the time on my wristwatch.
Then I ran to show Mr. Reilly,
but I was in such a hurry
that I *dropped* my tooth . . .
between the tetherball pole
and the hopscotch lines.

My stomach fluttered up and down.
I wiped my eyes with my mittens.
My lost tooth was *lost*!
How could I ever find it?

The blacktop looked so big,
with all those clumps of snow . . .
and my tooth was so small.

Tuck and Claire called the rest of the class,
and everyone got down on
their hands and knees
to help look for my lost tooth.
Even Mr. Reilly.
We were like detectives
searching for a tiny clue.

“Here it is, Lucy!” someone yelled.
“No, I found it!” called someone else.
“Over here! I found Lucy’s tooth!”

But each time,
my lost tooth turned out to be
just a pebble of ice or a dab of snow.

Then . . .

“. . . FOUND it!
I really FOUND it!
Whoooooopeeeee!”

Ian stood up
next to the 8 on the hopscotch lines,
carefully holding my tooth
between his thumb and his finger.

I rushed over to take a look.
“*Thank you*, Ian!
Mr. Reilly, come see!
It’s really my tooth!”

Mr. Reilly and all the second graders
crowded around us and cheered.

The End

Later
on the bus going home from school,
I thought about
my lost-but-found tooth
in my backpack.

Mr. Reilly was right.

Around the world
there were *thousands*
of second-grade tooth stories.

And *my* story . . .
was a good one.

LUCY FEBRUARY 27 12:25 P.M.

LOST AND FOUND
AT RECESS

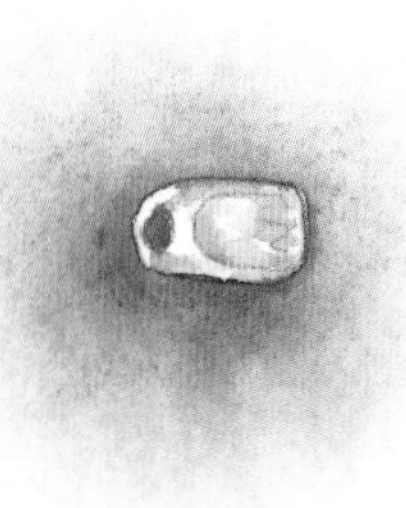